W9-COL-606

I Wish I Were A Butterfly

By James Howe

Illustrated by Ed Young

Voyager Books • **Harcourt, Inc.**

Orlando   Austin   New York   San Diego   Toronto   London

Manufactured in China

Every story has a beginning.

This story began with a group of children at the Old Trail School in Bath, Ohio, in the fall of 1985. With sparkling eyes and waving hands and giggles of delight, they invented the tale of a cricket who thought he was ugly and a toad who made him feel that way. The story was brief, and we moved on to other things.

But I took the idea away with me and coaxed from it a middle and an end. This book is dedicated to those kindergarten, first-, and second-graders, who are older now and may not remember. I share with them the excitement of what can come of a brief moment of invention. And I thank them for what is often the hardest part of telling any story—the beginning.

—J. H.

To the late Elizabeth Armstrong, who persuaded me to play a part beyond my first book

—E. Y.

For most of the crickets in Swampswallow Pond, sunrise was a happy time. They came out of their tunnel-dark homes and celebrated the light of day with a fiddler's song.

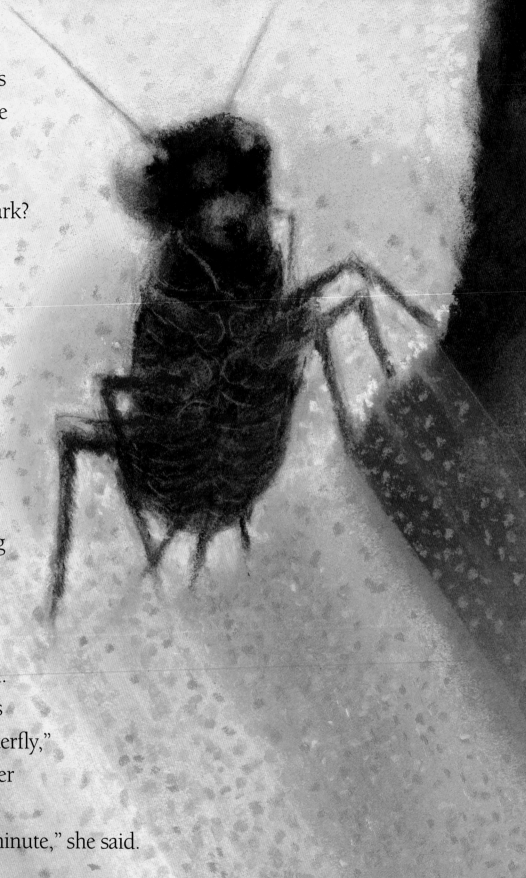

But the littlest cricket was sad. "I want to stay here," he told his mother.

"In the dark?" she asked. "What will you do in the dark? You must come outside to make music."

"Then I won't make music," said the littlest cricket defiantly. "I don't have anything to sing about anyway."

"You don't want to come outside. You don't want to make music. The next thing you know," his mother scolded, "you *won't* want to be a cricket."

The littlest cricket sighed. Had his mother guessed his secret? "I wish I were a butterfly," he said softly. But his mother didn't hear.

"Outside with you this minute," she said.

The littlest cricket knew better than to argue. Out into the bright daylight he went.

But he did not make any music.

The sound of the other crickets fiddling was more than he could bear. "Why are they so happy being crickets?" he asked out loud. "Perhaps they don't know what I do."

"And what is it that you know?" asked a passing glowworm.

The littlest cricket said, "I know that I am ugly. All crickets are ugly."

"Who told you such a thing?" the glowworm asked.

"The frog who lives at the edge of the pond. He told me that I am the ugliest creature he ever saw."

"Well," said the glowworm, inspecting the littlest cricket with care, "you are not the handsomest thing in the world, but you are far from the ugliest. Look at me, I'm no beauty myself."

"But you will change into a lightning bug," the littlest cricket said, "while I will always be a cricket. An ugly, ugly cricket. I wish I were a butterfly."

"There's no use wishing for what can't be," said the glowworm, going on his way. "Being a cricket seems fine enough to me."

"That's easy for him to say," said the littlest cricket. "He will be a lightning bug one day. And the frog who lives at the edge of the pond will never find *him* ugly."

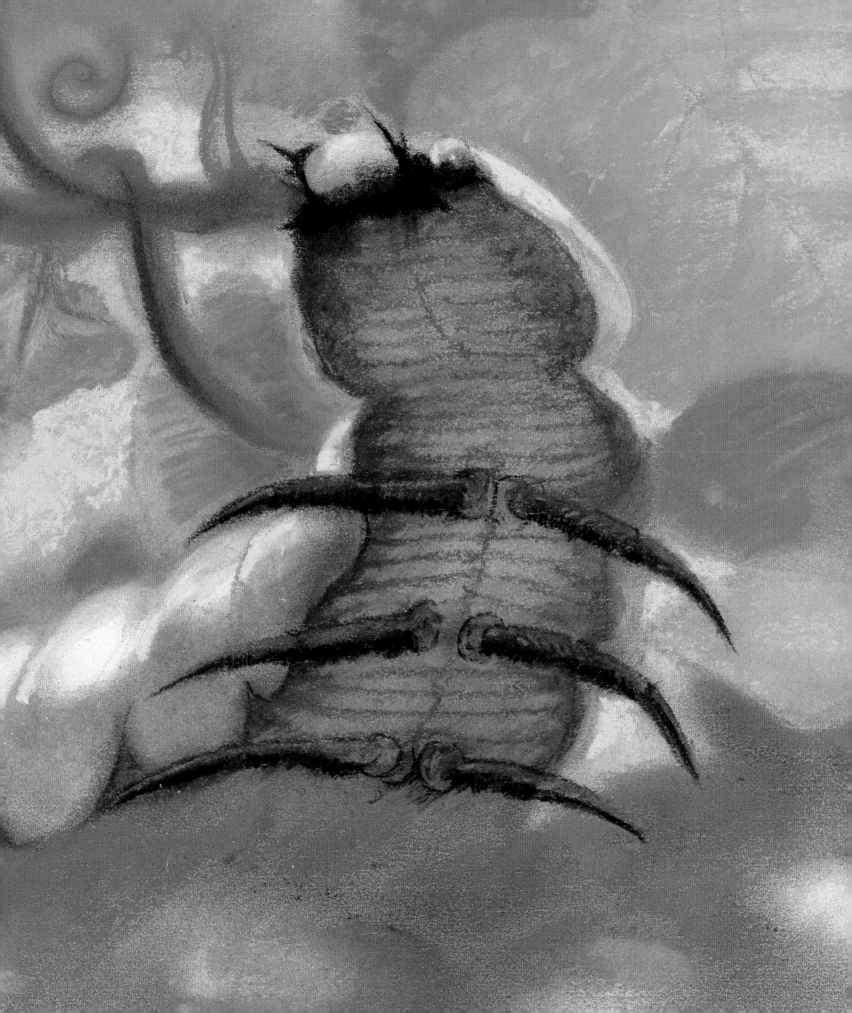

"What do you care what the frog who lives
at the edge of the pond has to say?" a
ladybug asked from atop a daisy. "If he told me
I was ugly, I wouldn't care one bit."

"But who would ever say *you* are ugly?" asked the
littlest cricket. "Everyone can see how lovely
you are. I am the color of a lump of dirt,
but you . . . you are the color of laughter,
if such a thing could be."

This amused the ladybug. "Perhaps you are right,"
she said. "But then you must learn to be
content with what you are and not mind
what a silly old frog tells you."

"That is easy for *you* to say," said the littlest
cricket as the ladybug flew away.
"Oh, I wish I were a butterfly."

He jumped onto a lily pad and drifted across the pond.

I'll talk to the Old One, he thought. She'll help me.

But seeing his reflection in the water, the littlest cricket started to cry.

"Why am I so ugly?" he asked his mirrored self. "Why can't I be—?"

"A dragonfly like me?"

The cricket looked up to see a dragonfly darting about overhead. "I couldn't help but hear your moaning and groaning," said the dragonfly. "It isn't right to be envious of others, you know. It's true that I am a magnificent creature, but so are you in your own way, I am sure."

"Hmph," said the littlest cricket. "You fly around with your whispery wings and your body all covered with jewels and tell me that *I* am magnificent? Please, Mister Dragonfly, go away. You don't understand. You can't understand. I wish I were a butterfly."

"Well, you're not a butterfly and never shall be," the dragonfly said firmly. "And wishing is a waste of time."

The littlest cricket blinked, and the dragonfly was gone. It's easy to be happy, he thought, when you are a glistening dragonfly. It's easy to be happy if you are *anything* but an ugly cricket like me.

In the middle of her web on
the other side of Swampswallow
Pond, the Old One was waiting. "I am good
at waiting," she had told the cricket once. "That is
a spider's life—spinning and waiting, waiting and spinning."

Today, when the Old One saw the littlest cricket
hop off the lily pad, she could see how sad he was. "It's a lovely day,"
the Old One called out. "And lovely days are too short to wear long faces.
What's wrong, my friend?"

"I am ugly," said the littlest cricket.

"Whoever told you that?" asked the spider.

"The frog who lives at the edge of the pond. I am the ugliest thing that ever lived. Oh, how I wish I were a butterfly."

The Old One began to laugh. "Butterflies are pretty enough to look at," she said, "but they are no more special than you."

"Not special?" cried the littlest cricket. "They are the most beautiful creatures in Swampswallow Pond and maybe in all the world. I wish I were as special as that."

The Old One said nothing, but continued to laugh.

"I thought *you* would understand," the cricket said. "You don't envy the butterfly because you're so beautiful yourself."

The spider stopped laughing at once.
"You think that I am beautiful?" she asked.

The cricket nodded.

"But I've been told that I'm the ugliest
creature in Swampswallow Pond, maybe in all
the world."

The cricket looked surprised. "Did the frog who lives at the edge of
the pond tell you that?"

"Not only the frog," said the Old One. "Why, if I were to believe what
everyone says about me, I would think myself quite, quite ugly. But I don't
believe everyone, you see. And I certainly don't believe
that grumpy old frog who lives at the edge of the pond.
I believe you because you are my friend.
You think I'm beautiful, and so I am."

"You *are* beautiful," the littlest cricket said.
"But I am as ugly as can be. I still wish
I were a butterfly."

The Old One asked the littlest cricket to follow her to the water's edge.

"Look," she said. "What do you see?"

"A beautiful you and an ugly me," replied the cricket. "What do *you* see?"

"Two beautiful friends."

The cricket gazed at himself for a long time. "Am I *really* beautiful?" he asked at last.

"To me you are," the Old One said. "More beautiful than any butterfly I've ever seen."

The littlest cricket looked back at his reflection and, to his surprise, his ugliness began to fade away.

Suddenly, a gust of wind rippled the water.

"Look," said the cricket, turning around. "Your web—the wind has blown away your web."

"Ah, well," the spider said, "then I must begin again. Wait and spin, spin and wait—it's a spider's life. But it would make the time pass more quickly if I had some music to work to."

As the Old One began to spin a new web, the littlest cricket began to fiddle.

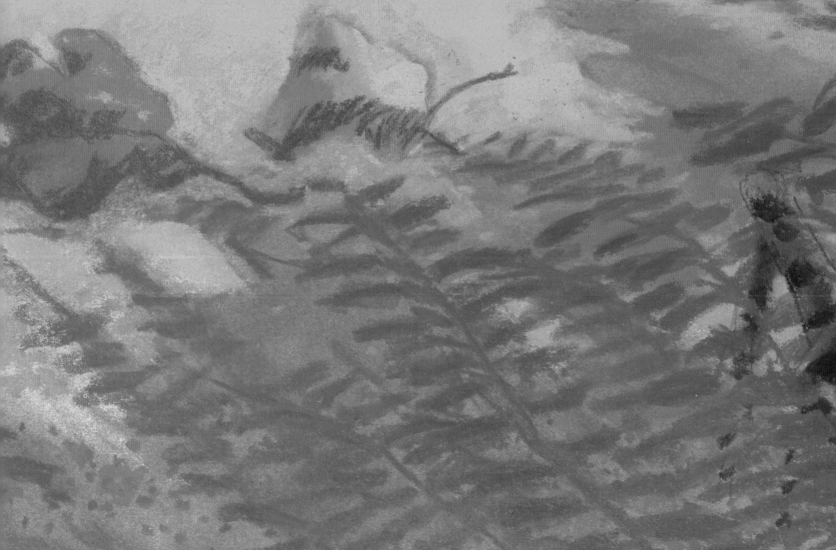

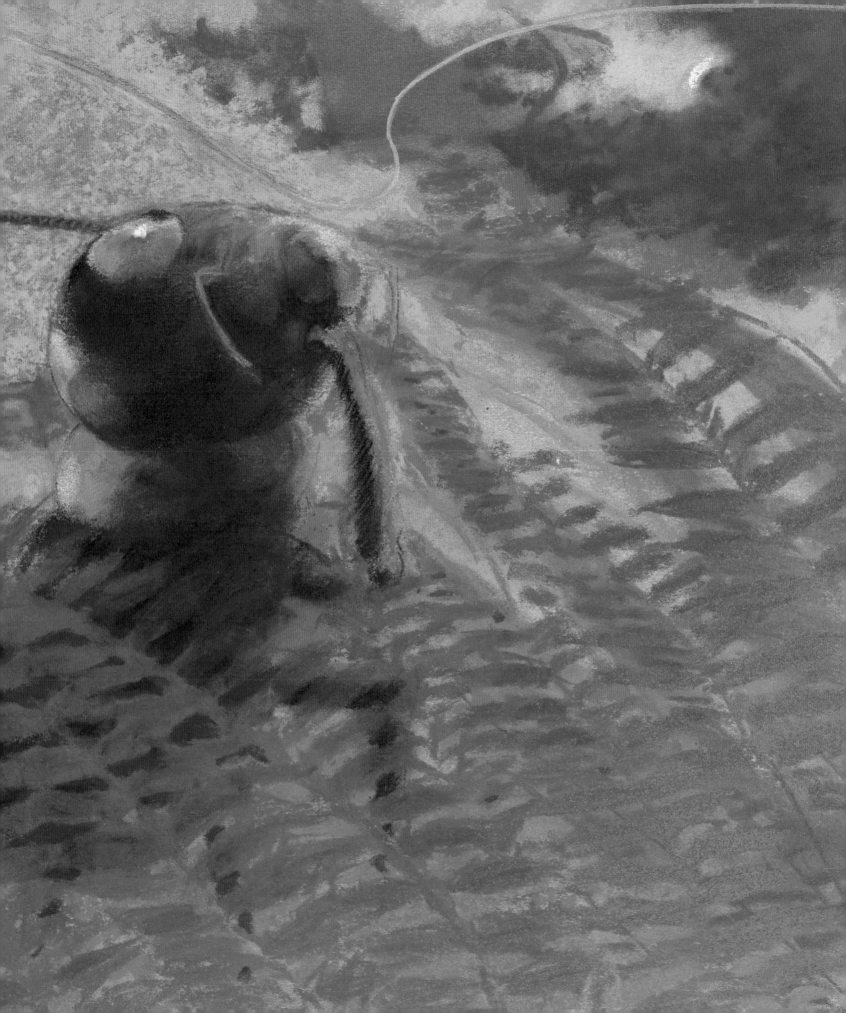

And a butterfly, flying past, heard the sound and said, "What beautiful music that creature makes. I wish I were a cricket."

Requests for permission to make copies of
any part of the work should be mailed to the
following address: Permissions Department,
Harcourt, Inc., 6277 Sea Harbor Drive,
Orlando, Florida 32887-6777.

Voyager Books is a registered
trademark of Harcourt, Inc.

Library of Congress Cataloging-in-Publication Data
Howe, James.
I wish I were a butterfly.
Summary: A wise spider helps a despondent
cricket realize that he is special in his own way.
[1. Friendship—Fiction.   2. Self-acceptance—
Fiction. 3. Crickets—Fiction.]
I. Young, Ed, ill. II. Title.
PZ7.H83727Iad   1987   [E]   86-33635
ISBN 0-15-200470-X
ISBN 0-15-238013-2 pb

P Q R S T U V

The illustrations in this book were done in pastel on 200 lb. Stonehenge paper.
The display type was hand-lettered by Judythe Sieck.
The text type was set in ITC Berkeley Old Style Book
by Thompson Type, San Diego, California.
Printed by South China Printing Co. Ltd., China
Production supervision by Warren Wallerstein and Eileen McGlone
Designed by Joy Chu